SCIENCE SKILLS

WHAT DO YOU KNOW ABOUT PLANTS?

ANGELA ROYSTON

PowerKiDS
press

Published in 2018 by **The Rosen Publishing Group, Inc.**
29 East 21st Street, New York, NY 10010

CATALOGING-IN-PUBLICATION DATA
Names: Royston, Angela.
Title: What do you know about plants? / Angela Royston.
Description: New York : PowerKids Press, 2018. | Series: Test your science skills | Includes index.
Identifiers: ISBN 9781538323106 (pbk.) | ISBN 9781538322154 (library bound) | ISBN 9781538323113 (6 pack)
Subjects: LCSH: Plants--Juvenile literature. | Plants--Miscellanea--Juvenile literature.
Classification: LCC QK49.R68 2018 | DDC 580--dc23

Copyright © 2018 Franklin Watts, a division of Hachette Children's Group

Series Editor: Amy Pimperton
Series Designer: Emma DeBanks
Picture Researcher: Diana Morris

Picture credits: aaabbbccc/Shutterstock: 12t. ajt/Shutterstock: 27cr. Andriano/Shutterstock: 7bl, 29b. AP/PAI: 20b. Artistas/Shutterstock: 14c. art-partner images/Getty Images: 21b. Bonnie Taylor Barry/Shutterstock: 22bl. Radu Bercan/Shutterstock: 19c. Billion Photos/Shutterstock: 15c. Biofoto Associates/SPL: 18c. Gary Blakeley/Shutterstock 17b. ByEmo/Shutterstock: 11br. Nigel Catlin/FLPA: 8t. Chainfoto24/Shutterstock: 12c. Paul Crash/Shutterstock: 3bc. Stefan Diller/SPL: 15b. Neil Donoghue/Shutterstock: 11bl. Dreamy Girl/Shutterstock: 22t. Eye of Science/SPL: 14t. fotomirk/Shutterstock: 27c. Olga Glinskaja/Shutterstock: 21c. Hhelene/Shutterstock: 9t. Jeremy Sutton-Hibbert/ Alamy: 27b. Homey Design/Shutterstock: 23ca. Jiang Hongyan/Shutterstock: 17t. Bjørn Hovdal/Deamstime: 27t. iko/Shutterstock: 6t. javarman/Shutterstock: 5b. Kichigin/Shutterstock: 8b. Igor Kovalchuk/Shutterstock: 25t. R Lan/ Shutterstock: 21t. Katrina Leigh/Shutterstock: 9b. Libra/Shutterstock: 19t. Likar/Shutterstock: 24t. Little_Desire/ Shutterstock: 25b. Louisebittersweet/Dreamstime: 18b. tea maeklong/Shutterstock: 18t. majaan/Shutterstock: 22br. Anna Minsk/Shutterstock: 26b. Miny/Shutterstock: 23c. msgrafixx/Shutterstock: 10t. Maks Narodenko/ Shutterstock: 17c. Njene/Shutterstock: 3br, 24b. Noppharat4569/Shutterstock: 4t. Oshcan/Getty Images: front cover. Natalya Osipova/Shutterstock: 26c. pixinoo/Shutterstock: 6b. pogonici/Shutterstock: 16t, 28b. Valentina Razumova/ Shutterstock: 23b. Werner Rebel/Shutterstock: 4b. Peter Roeder/Dreamstime: 20c. Rssooli/Shutterstock: 14b. Sakarin Sawasdinaka/Shutterstock: 27cl. ScripX/Shutterstock: 13b. Dipak Shelare/Shutterstock: 11t. Andrei Shumskiy/ Shutterstock: 7r, 19b, 29t. Gary K Smith/FLPA: 26t. Olaf Speier/Shutterstock: 20t. Stockr/Shutterstock: 12b. Navakun Suwantragul/Shutterstock: 10b, 29c. Syda productions/Shutterstock: 16cl. Irinia Tischenko/Shutterstock: 25tc. Tim UR/Shutterstock: 23t. vetasster/Shutterstock: 15t. Frank Vicentz/CC Wikimedia: 10c. Wam1975/Dreamstime: 1. wawritto/Shutterstock: 5t. WHA/Photoshot: 16cr. winnond/Shutterstock: 6c.

Every attempt has been made to clear copyright. Should there be any inadvertent omission please apply to the publisher for rectification.

Manufactured in China
CPSIA Compliance Information: Batch BW18PK: For Further Information contact Rosen Publishing, New York, New York at 1-800-237-9932.

CONTENTS

Words in **bold** can be found in the glossary on page 30.

A note about measurements
Measurements are given in U.S. form with
metric in parentheses. The metric conversion
is rounded to make it easier to measure.

WHAT MAKES A PLANT A PLANT?

Plants are living things that have roots, a trunk or stem, leaves, and the ability to produce seeds, cones, or spores that will grow into new plants.

Plants include trees and bushes, which have wooden trunks and branches. Other plants are **vines**, flowers, grasses, ferns, and mosses.

Conifer trees, such as pines, have needles instead of broad leaves and produce new seeds in cones. Many other plants have flowers in which new seeds develop, while ferns and mosses grow from **spores**, not seeds.

Brown clusters of spores form under the fronds of a fern.

POLLINATION

A flower produces a new seed when one of its female eggs, or **ovules**, combines with a grain of male **pollen** from another flower of the same type. This is called pollination. Colorful flowers rely on insects (particularly bees) or birds to carry the pollen from flower to flower.

Grasses and many trees have small green flowers whose pollen is blown through the air by the wind. Spores are also spread by the wind.

pollen

Grasses produce many small flowers at the top of tall stems. The wind blows clouds of pollen from the flowers.

PHOTOSYNTHESIS

The most important feature that plants share is their ability to make food. The process is called **photosynthesis**, and it mostly takes place in the leaves. Water taken in through the roots is combined with **carbon dioxide** from the air to make sugar.

This **chemical reaction** could not happen without **chlorophyll**, a green substance contained in the leaves. Chlorophyll takes in energy from light and then releases the energy to power the chemical reaction. The sugar travels from the leaves along thin **veins** to feed every part of the plant.

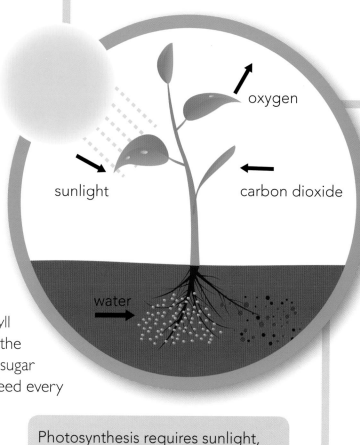

oxygen

sunlight

carbon dioxide

water

Photosynthesis requires sunlight, the gas carbon dioxide, and water.

VITAL PLANTS

Animals, including humans, could not survive without plants. Some animals feed directly on plants, and others feed on these plant-eating animals. If you trace what each animal in a **food chain** eats, the chain always begins with plants. Plants also keep the air we breathe stocked with **oxygen**. Photosynthesis produces oxygen as a waste gas, which is released into the air. Animals use oxygen to change food into energy, and cannot survive without it.

A cheetah is a meat-eater that hunts wildebeest and other animals. Wildebeest feed on grass and other plant leaves.

THE SCIENCE OF PLANTS

Plants are incredibly useful to scientists. Plants contain chemicals and materials that scientists explore and test to see how they can be used.

Many everyday products, from toothpaste to T-shirts, contain ingredients that come from plants. New plants are being discovered all the time, and some have unique properties, such as the ability to cure particular diseases.

Fluffy cotton **bolls** protect the cotton plant seeds inside. Bolls are turned into cotton fibers to make clothing.

Medicines made from the Madagascar periwinkle are used to treat cancer.

PERFECT PLANTS

Plants are perfect subjects to investigate. Unlike animals, they cannot run away and they do not feel pain. It is easy to grow the large numbers of plants that scientists need to conduct experiments. This helps scientists check that the same **outcome** always occurs. Experiments are often repeated with small changes to see how the change affects the outcome.

You can experiment with plants too. This book includes experiments that test what plants need to grow, and whether plants prefer one kind of liquid or color of light to another. You can explore why leaves change color in the fall, and you can even **clone** some plants.

Modern farming allows thousands of plants to be grown in nurseries.

WORKING SCIENTIFICALLY

In this book, you'll find a range of experiments or investigations that will help you discover how plants work.

To do experiments, scientists use careful, logical methods to make sure they get reliable results. The experiments in this book use four key steps to the scientific method, along with an easy acronym to help you remember them: ATOM.

 ## ASK

What do you want to find out?

Asking questions is a really important part of science. Scientists think about what questions they have, and how to find the answers.

 ## TEST

Setting up an experiment that will test ideas and answer questions

Scientists then design experiments to answer their questions. A test works best if you only test for one thing at a time.

 ## OBSERVE

Key things to look out for

Scientists watch their experiments closely to see what is happening.

 ## MEASURE

Measuring and recording results, such as temperatures, sizes, or amounts of time

Making accurate measurements and recording the results shows what the experiment has revealed.

WHAT NEXT?

After each experiment, the What Next? section gives you ideas for more activities and experiments, or ways to display your results.

SEEDS

A seed contains a store of food and an undeveloped plant called an **embryo**. When the seed takes in water, it swells and the embryo begins to grow. It uses the food stored in the seed while its roots grow down into the soil. This is called germination.

As it takes in water from the soil through its roots, the shoot grows up through the soil into the light. When the shoot's first two leaves open, they can begin to photosynthesize (see page 5).

food store

embryo

root

This bean has been cut in half to show how a new plant begins to grow.

SPEEDY AND SLOW

Some plants grow from seeds faster than others. The seeds of **weeds** and wild flowers, such as dandelions and chickweed, grow almost at once. Some desert flowers lie **dormant** as seeds in the ground and wait for months or years for a heavy shower of rain. Then the seeds grow quickly into plants with flowers and make new seeds before the ground dries up again.

The seeds of wild flowers, such as these daisies, take root and grow quickly on a patch of land.

SCIENCE EXPERIMENT:
THE SEED RACE

Plant different types of seeds to find out which germinates first and which grows fastest.

runner bean seeds

ASK

Which type of seed will grow the fastest? Which will be the first to sprout?

TEST

• Fill each tray with soil so it is about 1 inch (3 cm) deep.
• Add water to make the soil damp.
• Label one tray "peas." Plant each pea seed 2 inches (5 cm) apart, just below the surface.
• Label and plant the runner beans in the other tray.
• Place the trays in a warm, dark place.

OBSERVE

When the first seeds in a tray sprout, place the tray near a well-lit window. Check both trays every day. Add water to keep the soil damp.

MEASURE

Every four days, measure the height of the tallest seedling in each tray. Draw a graph for each type of seed. Which seed grew fastest and won the race?

WHAT NEXT?

About three weeks after they sprout, carefully scoop the seedlings from their trays and plant them in small plant pots filled with extra soil so they can continue to grow. Once the plants are big enough, plant them in a vegetable patch in your garden.

A seedling unfurls its first two leaves and grows more roots in the first few days after germination.

PLANT DEFENSE

Many plants have developed different ways of protecting themselves from being eaten. Some plants have sharp thorns or spiky leaves, while others contain **toxins** that are harmful if eaten. A few plants combine spikes with poisonous **acids**.

A nettle is covered with tiny hair-like stingers, which contain **formic acid**. When you touch a hair, the tip of the stinger breaks off and the acid shoots into your skin, causing an itchy, painful rash.

A nettle's tiny stingers contain poison, which protects the plant from being eaten or attacked by animals.

WHAT IS AN ACID?

Acids are chemicals that are **corrosive** and **neutralize alkalies**. Alkalies are chemicals that are also corrosive and neutralize acids. Scientists test for acids and alkalies using universal indicator paper and a scale, which gives a **pH value** between 0 and 14. Acids turn the paper red, orange, or yellow and measure between 0 and 7, with 0 being the most acidic. Alkalies turn the paper green, blue or purple and measure between 7 and 14.

universal indicator paper

alkali

acid

YOU WILL NEED:

- 5 plastic cups
  - Labels
  - Gloves
- Freshly picked nettles
- Lemon juice, milk, vinegar
  - Window cleaner
  - Measuring cup
  - 5 teaspoons
- Universal indicator paper
  - Kitchen towel

SCIENCE EXPERIMENT:
ACID TEST

Many foods and everyday products are acidic. How does the acid in a nettle compare with them?

Ask an adult to supervise you when using glass cleaner or other household products.

Wash your hands after you have done this experiment.

 ASK

Is a nettle more or less acidic than the other four everyday substances you will test?

TEST

- Label each cup with one of the substances.
- Wearing gloves, crush four or five nettle leaves in the "nettle" cup with a teaspoon.
- Pour 1.7 ounces (50 ml) of water into each plastic cup.
- Using a clean spoon each time, mix a teaspoon of each liquid you are testing into its plastic cup.
- Dip a strip of universal indicator paper into the first cup and leave for 20 seconds. Remove the paper and place it on a clean piece of kitchen towel.
- Repeat the last step with each remaining cup in turn.

 OBSERVE

Note how quickly the universal indicator paper changes color. Which strip is the reddest?

MEASURE

Use this universal indicator chart to match the color of each strip to its pH value. Draw a bar chart to show how the nettle compares with the other liquids.

Universal indicator chart

Acid   Alkali

0   7   14

pH Value

Products that contain strong acids or alkalies usually carry a warning sign to show that they are dangerous and should be handled carefully.

WHAT NEXT?

Test some more household items to work out their acid or alkali pH values, such as toothpaste, liquid soap, and tap water.

WHAT PLANTS NEED TO GROW

Plants need the right conditions to grow well. These conditions include temperature, soil type, and amount of light. Some plants need to be in a sunny place, while others, such as rainforest plants, prefer a shady place.

Poppies grow well in bright sunshine.

WATER

Most of all, plants need water. Most plants rely on rainwater to keep their soils moist. **Tropical** rainforest plants get rain almost every day.

Rainforest plants get so much rain they grow very close together. Some grow very tall.

FERTILIZERS

Soil contains nutrients, such as nitrogen, phosphorus, and potassium. Plants use these chemicals from the soil to photosynthesize, breathe, and grow. **Fertilizers** contain extra nutrients, so farmers add them to the soil to help their crops grow even better.

This farmer is spraying fertilizer onto the soil so that his plants will produce a bigger crop.

ADDED EXTRAS

The liquids we drink are mostly made up of water that contains other things. Fruit juice and soda contain sugar, and milk contains fats and proteins. Will plants grow better when they are "watered" with our drinks?

 ASK

Which liquid will most help a plant to grow?

 TEST

- Measure 3 ounces (100 ml) of water and pour it into the bowl of one of the plants.
- Repeat with the other liquids and plants.
- Label each bowl with its liquid.
- Place the bowls and pots on a sunny windowsill.

 OBSERVE

Check the plants every few hours to see which plant begins to flop first. Look closely at the leaves and stems. Keep checking for a few days and record what happens to each plant.

 MEASURE

Measure the height of each plant every day. Draw a graph to show how each plant grew. Did you predict correctly?

WHAT NEXT?

Use the drinks' packaging to check the amount of sugar in each liquid. Check the pH level of each liquid (see pages 10–11). Does this help you explain the outcome?

When plants don't have enough to "drink," the stems droop and the leaves shrivel up as the plant dries out.

SURVIVING A DROUGHT

Plants take in water through tiny hairs on their roots. The water moves through the roots into narrow tubes, or **xylem**, in the stem. From the stem, water travels to every leaf, bud, flower, or fruit. You can see some xylem if you examine a stalk of celery. The tubes end in stringy pieces at the bottom of the stalk.

The dark green dots on this thin slice of celery stem are the plant's xylem.

WATER IN FLOWERS

When a flower has finished its job of fertilizing seeds, it wilts. The plant cuts the water supply to the flowers and the petals crumple, shrink, and fall off. The fruits and seeds can then take in more water and begin to swell and ripen.

LOW ON WATER

You can see how important water is to a plant by watching what happens when it is low on water. The plant loses its rigidity — the flowers and leaves droop, dry up, and fall off. In some plants the whole stem droops too. In extreme cases, the plant may die.

Pea plants produce pods of seeds (peas). The pod protects the seeds as they swell and ripen.

These crops are wilting because there is a drought — a long period of time when there is little to no rain.

SCIENCE EXPERIMENT:
THIRSTY PLANTS

Some plants can survive without water better than others. Test different plants and compare what happens as they dry up and then are watered again.

 ASK

Which plant will survive the longest without water?

 TEST

- Place each herb in an empty cup and wait until it wilts. (Some may wilt quickly, so check the plants two or three times each day.)
- When each herb wilts, pour 3 ounces (100 ml) of water into its cup

Rosemary   Mint   Parsley   Basil

 OBSERVE

Note how long each herb lasts before it wilts. What happens when you water it again?

 MEASURE

Record whether each herb recovers when you water it and how long it takes. Draw bar charts to compare how well the herbs lasted without water and how quickly they recovered.

WHAT NEXT?

Compare the stems of each herb to see whether there is a link between the rigidity or bendiness of the stem and the results. Repeat the experiment with plants that have flowers, such as a rose. Do you get the same result?

This picture shows a close up of the xylem in a rosemary stem.

WATER CONTENT

Water content is the amount of water something contains. The water content of fruit and vegetables is between 80 and 95%. A quick way to check water content is to test whether something sinks or floats in water. The faster it sinks, the less water it contains.

Most oranges contain about 2 ounces (70 ml) of juice.

A pepper floats because it is filled with air, which is lighter than water.

DENSITY

Density is a more accurate way to measure water content. The density of water is 1 gram per **cubic centimeter** (1 g/cc). An object that floats is less dense or has the same density as water. An object that sinks is denser than water.

Density is calculated by dividing the weight of an object by its volume, but how do you measure the volume of fruits and vegetables that have irregular shapes? An ancient Greek scientist called Archimedes solved the problem. He sank the object in a container filled with water and measured the volume of water that spilled over.

Archimedes' great idea came to him in the bath! He realized that the volume of water displaced as he submerged himself was the same as the volume of his body.

YOU WILL NEED:

- A tomato, a potato, a chunk of carrot, and a chunk of cucumber
- Kitchen scales
- A measuring cup
- A drinking straw
- Notebook and pen

SCIENCE EXPERIMENT:
SINK OR FLOAT?

You can use Archimedes' method to calculate whether various fruits and vegetables are more or less dense than water and to calculate their volume.

ASK

Which items will float? Will any sink? Which one do you predict has the lowest water content?

TEST

- Weigh each fruit or vegetable and write down its weight.
- Pour water into the cup up to the 20 ounce (600 cc) mark.
- Carefully place the tomato in the water.
- If it floats, push it below the surface with the straw.
- Read the water level on the cup and write it down.
- Repeat with the other items.

OBSERVE

Which fruits and vegetables float and which sink? Were your predictions correct?

WHAT NEXT?

Repeat the experiment using an orange, a banana, an apple, and a parsnip. See if you can find out why heavy, metal ships are able to float on water without sinking to the bottom of the ocean.

MEASURE

Use the two measurements of water level in the cup to calculate the volume of each fruit or vegetable. Divide the weight of each by its volume to get the density. The fruit or vegetable with the highest density has the lowest water content.

a huge container ship

HOW LEAVES WORK

Leaves are food factories — they manufacture a sugary, liquid sap that feeds the whole plant. Only green plants can make their own food and their leaves are brilliantly structured to photosynthesize sugar from carbon dioxide and water.

The lines on a leaf are called veins. They consist of bundles of tubes that bring water into the leaf and carry away the sugary sap.

stomata

STRUCTURE OF A LEAF

Tiny **pores** in the leaf, called **stomata**, open to let carbon dioxide from the air into the leaf and oxygen gas out. The leaf sucks up water through the roots and xylem. Green chlorophyll absorbs energy from sunlight, and this drives the reaction that turns carbon dioxide and water into sugar. The surface of the leaf is protected by a tough, transparent layer, which allows sunlight through.

LEAVES LOVE SUNLIGHT!

Leaves are flat and thin to give a large area for sunlight to strike. A plant moves its leaves so that the flat surfaces face the Sun. As the Sun moves across the sky, the leaves turn to follow the Sun.

Sunflowers slowly turn to face the Sun and soak up as much sunlight as they can.

BLOCKING OUT THE LIGHT

Explore what happens to a leaf when light cannot reach all or part of the leaf.

YOU WILL NEED:

- 3 different potted plants
- Sticky notes and scissors
- Notebook and pen
- Color chart for greens and yellows (you can use the one shown on this page)

 ASK

What happens to the chlorophyll in a leaf when it is deprived of light?

 TEST

- Use the color chart to note each plant's leaf color.
- Cut the sticky notes into different sizes and shapes, and make some that cover a whole leaf of each plant.
- Stick the shapes to some of the leaves of each plant. Stick some on top of the leaf; stick some underneath.
- Carefully remove the shapes after a week.

 OBSERVE

What has happened to the patches of leaf below the shapes? Did it make a difference if the shape was on top of, or underneath, the leaf?

WHAT NEXT?

Record how long it takes for each leaf to return to its original color.

MEASURE

Match the color of the patches to the colors on the charts. Count the number of patches for each color. Are the colors different for each plant?

HELPING NATURE?

Plants grow best in the summer, when the weather is warm and the days are long and bright. In the winter, the weather is colder, the days are shorter, and the light is dimmer. How can farmers change a crop's environment so that the crop produces a bigger, better harvest?

These farm crops are growing under and through long sheets of polythene.

WARM AND BRIGHT

Some farmers cover vegetable crops with huge polythene sheets, which trap heat and protect the crops from frost. Growing plants indoors or in greenhouses can be expensive, but it allows farmers to give plants extra light as well as heat. Using **artificial** light means that plants can photosynthesize and grow, even when it is dark outside.

Plants grow fast in this special farm building, lit day and night by pink lights.

TESTING COLORS

Sunlight looks white, but it actually contains all the colors of the rainbow. Do plants use all of the colors it contains? This experiment tests whether some colors help plants grow better than others.

YOU WILL NEED:

- 4 plants of the same type in separate pots
- 3 rolls of colored cellophane
- 1 roll of clear cellophane
- 4 sticks about 12 inches (30 cm) long
- Scissors
- Sticky tape

 ## ASK

Which color or colors of light will help a plant grow most?

 ## OBSERVE

Check the plants every day. Do you notice any changes?

 ## MEASURE

Measure the height of each plant at the beginning of the experiment, and then measure the height again after a week. Draw a bar chart to compare the heights for each color.

 ## TEST

- Cut 20 x 20 inch (50 x 50 cm) squares of each color of cellophane.
- Mark the center of each square by folding into quarters. Cut a small hole at the center.
- Push a stick into the soil in each plant pot.
- Slide a square of cellophane over each stick until the plant is covered. Tape the cellophane to the stick and tuck in the sides to keep ordinary light out.
- Put the plant pots in a brightly lit place, such as a windowsill.

cellophane

WHAT NEXT?

Remove the cellophane. How long does it take for any or all of the plants to recover?

A glass **prism** can be used to show how white light splits into all of the colors of the rainbow.

FLOWERS AND SEEDS

An ovule becomes a **fertilized** seed when a grain of pollen from another flower combines with it. The male parts of a flower produce pollen, while the female parts receive pollen and pass it to the ovules.

POLLEN TO SEED

The stigma, style, ovary and ovules are the female parts of the flower. When a ripe pollen grain lands on a style, it grows a narrow tube down the style to an ovule below. The pollen then moves down the tube and joins with the ovule. The ovule develops into a seed as the ovary swells into a fruit.

stigma

style

pollen

ovules

pollen tube

ovary

Each grain of pollen grows a tube to reach an ovule in the ovary.

Birds help to scatter the seeds inside these juicy berry fruits.

sycamore seed

SEEDS

Seeds develop better when they fall onto soil some distance from the plant. Many plants, such as sycamore trees, rely on the wind to distribute their seeds. Peas develop in pods that split and catapult their seeds out. Other plants wrap their seeds in juicy fruits. Animals eat the fruits and then drop the seeds or deposit them in their droppings, often far away.

GROWING STRAWBERRIES

You can observe how pollination works and a flower produces a fruit and seeds by growing strawberries in pots or in a window box.

ASK

Which plant will produce the most strawberries?

TEST

- Plant the strawberry plants in a window box and place it outside or on a window sill.
- Label the plants A and B and water them to keep the soil moist.
- When the plants flower, use a paintbrush to gently move pollen from the flowers of plant A to the flowers of plant B (but be careful not to move pollen from plant B to plant A). Use a different brush for each flower.
- Pick the strawberries as they become ripe.

OBSERVE

Watch the plants grow. Record the date when the experiment started, when the flowers bud, when they open and when they wilt. Does one plant produce more or fewer strawberries? Why do you think this might be?

MEASURE

Make a table to record how long it takes for the strawberries to swell and ripen and to show how many strawberries each plant produces.

WHAT NEXT?

Look for the seeds on each strawberry. Most plants hide their seeds inside the fruit, but strawberries embed their seeds on the outside.

strawberry seeds

FALL COLORS

In the fall, maple leaves change color from green to orange to bright red, before they fall from the tree.

Colorful fall leaves show that winter is coming! Evergreen needles have a tough, waxy surface to protect them from freezing. Broad, flat leaves, however, would be damaged by frost, so the tree discards them.

WHAT CAUSES THE COLORS?

Green leaves get their color from chlorophyll, the chemical needed for photosynthesis (see page 5). As fall nights get colder, the leaves stop producing chlorophyll and the green fades, revealing shades of red, orange, and yellow. These colors were there all along, but only become visible in the fall.

Different chemicals in the leaves produce the different colors.

YOU WILL NEED:

- Soft leaves from 2 broad-leafed trees, such as maple and lime
- Rubbing alcohol
- Coffee filter paper and scissors
- Ruler
- 2 cups
- 2 pens
- Sticky tape

SCIENCE EXPERIMENT:

HIDDEN COLORS

You don't have to wait until fall to see the hidden colors in a green leaf. Try this experiment in late summer to reveal the colors below the chlorophyll.

lime leaf

ASK

Which leaf will reveal the brightest colors?

TEST

- Cut the maple leaves into tiny pieces and fill one of the cups a quarter of the way full with them.
- Repeat with the lime leaves. Label each cup with the name of its leaf.
- Ask an adult to pour in surgical spirit or rubbing alcohol to just cover the leaves, stir and leave them to soak for about 30 minutes.
- Cut two 1 x 4 inch (2 x 10 cm) strips from the coffee filter paper.
- Place a pen across each tumbler and stick a strip of filter paper to it so that the end of the strip just touches the liquid.
- When the liquid reaches the top of the strips, remove and leave to dry.

OBSERVE

Watch the liquid from the leaf mixture soak up the strip. Look for the colors that appear on the strip.

WHAT NEXT?

Repeat with different leaves, including a broad evergreen leaf, such as ivy.

MEASURE

When the strips are dry, measure the width of each band of color. Stick the strips to a larger piece of paper to display the results.

ivy leaf

CLONING PLANTS

Cloning is a way of producing new plants from a part of an existing plant. The new plants are then identical to the original plant, unlike plants grown from seeds, which grow into uniquely different plants.

NATURAL CLONING

Some plants, such as strawberries, can clone themselves. Strawberries produce stems called runners, which grow along the ground before putting down roots. Plants that grow from bulbs often clone themselves too. The bulbs split into two or more bulbs, which then grow into separate plants.

runner

A strawberry plant grows a runner that a new plant then grows from.

TAKING CUTTINGS

The easiest way to clone some plants is to take a **cutting** by snipping off a section of stem with leaves and putting it in water. After a while, the stem produces new roots and can be planted into soil.

cutting

roots

Geranium plants are easy to grow from cuttings.

YOU WILL NEED:

- A tray or shallow bowl
- Water
- Kitchen towel
- A carrot, a garlic clove, a leek, and a head of lettuce
- Notepad and pen
- Camera

SCIENCE EXPERIMENT:

WHAT CAN YOU CLONE?

You can clone a plant from its stem, its roots or a bulb, but some plants are easier to clone than others. Can you clone plants from pieces of vegetables?

clove of garlic

ASK

Which vegetable will grow into a whole new plant?

TEST

- Cut off the flat end of the carrot.
- Cut off the bottom of the leek and the bottom of the lettuce.
- Place two sheets of kitchen towel in the tray and cover with enough water to soak the paper.
- Put the vegetables and the clove of garlic on top of the kitchen roll.

leek

carrot

lettuce

OBSERVE

Check the tray every day and add water to keep the paper moist. Look for the appearance of tiny roots or shoots. Take a photograph every other day.

WHAT NEXT?

If any of your vegetables produce roots and shoots, plant them in a pot filled with soil and you may be able to grow a cloned plant.*

MEASURE

After a week, measure any roots or shoots that have grown. Which clone is most successful? Use your photos to make a display.

One of the most famous cloning experiments was the cloning of Dolly the Sheep. Scientists cloned her in 1995 from a single **cell**!

* see note on page 32.

READING YOUR RESULTS

When scientists do experiments, they get results. Even if nothing happened as they expected, that is a result too! All results can be useful, but it is important to understand them. Here are some guidelines that scientists use to learn from their results.

USE A CONTROL

In the Added Extras experiment (page 13), the control is the plant that you give the water to. A control is a normal version of the setup, without the things that are being tested — in this case the milk, orange juice and soda.

It's really important that apart from the thing being tested, the control version matches the test version in every way. So you use the same type of plant, size of pot, and amounts of soil and liquid as the other plants. Then you know that any differences in your results are purely down to the liquids.

REPEAT AND VERIFY

An experiment may work well once, but what if that was a fluke? So that they can be sure of their results, scientists often repeat an experiment several times to verify their results.

CHECK FOR BIAS

If you're *really* hoping for an exciting result, it's possible you might accidentally-on-purpose "help" your experiment along by ignoring something that doesn't fit with what you wanted. This is called "bias," and it can happen without you even realizing it.

OUTLIERS

What if you were conducting the Acid Test experiment (page 11) and the milk sample registered as more acidic than the vinegar?

You'd probably be quite surprised, because if you had a stomachache, you would be more likely to drink milk than vinegar! This unusual result is called an outlier and scientists have to check outliers carefully and work out why they have happened. For example, the milk might have gone sour, which increases its acidity.

KEEPING RECORDS

Writing down the details of each experiment and what the results were is essential for scientists. Not only does it help explain their work to others; it also means they can use results to look for patterns. For example, in the Hidden Colors experiment (page 25), is there a link between the colors produced and the colors of the leaves in fall?

MAKING MISTAKES

If you spot a mistake, start the experiment again. It would be an even bigger mistake to use the results from a badly run experiment.

However, if a mistake makes something interesting happen, you could set up a new experiment to test for that instead. Many important discoveries have been made this way. For example, artificial sweeteners were discovered by a chemist who forgot to wash his hands after handling coal and other chemicals. When he got home, he noticed his hands tasted sweet!

GLOSSARY

acid A substance that turns universal indicator paper red. Very strong acids can dissolve some metals.

alkali A substance that turns universal indicator paper blue and neutralizes acids.

artificial Not occurring naturally; human-made.

boll A type of round seed pod.

carbon dioxide One of the gases that make up the Earth's atmosphere.

cell The smallest structure in the body of a living thing; cells contain a nucleus.

chemical reaction When two or more chemicals combine to form a substance.

chlorophyll The green substance in plants that absorbs energy from light.

clone An identical copy.

corrosive Able to eat away or break up a substance.

cubic centimeter (cc) A cube that measures 1 cm high x 1 cm wide x 1 cm deep.

cutting Part of the stem or root of a plant, which can be used to grow an identical plant.

density The weight of an object, or its mass, compared to its volume.

dormant A plant that is alive, but not growing at that time.

embryo A tiny part inside a seed that grows into a new plant.

fertilized A seed that is able to grow, as male pollen has joined with a female ovule.

fertilizer A chemical or natural substance that is added to soil to help plants grow.

food chain A sequence of living things in which one eats the next, which eats the next, and so on.

formic acid An acid that is found in the stings of nettles, some other plants, and in the stings of some ants.

neutralize To cancel out. An alkali neutralizes an acid in the same way that cold water neutralizes hot water.

nitrogen A chemical that can be used as a nutrient to help plants and living things to grow.

outcome A result.

ovule A female egg inside a plant before it is fertilized.

oxygen A gas that most living things, including humans, need to take in to survive.

pH value A reading on a scale that shows how acidic or alkali something is.

phosphorus A chemical that plants use to help them grow.

photosynthesis The chemical reaction in plants that turns carbon dioxide, light, and water into the sugars that a plant feeds on.

pollen Fine, yellow dust grains that fertilize ovules.

pore A tiny hole in a leaf or in human skin that gases and liquids can pass through.

potassium A chemical that plants use to help them grow.

prism A 3-D geometric glass object with a triangular shape, used to split white light into the color rays of the spectrum.

spore A tiny body which, if the conditions are right, can develop into a new individual. Ferns, mosses, fungi, and bacteria all reproduce using spores.

stomata The tiny holes in a leaf through which carbon dioxide enters the leaf and oxygen leaves it.

toxin Poison produced by a plant or animal.

tropical Something that lives in the tropics, the hot, wet areas of the Earth above and below the Equator.

veins Tiny tubes that carry sugar and water in a leaf.

vine A plant with a long, woody stem that clings to and climbs up walls or trees.

weeds Wild flowers that grow in the wrong place, such as a garden, where they were not deliberately planted by humans.

xylem Tiny, tough tubes in a plant stem that carry water and nutrients from the soil and help to support the plant.

BOOKS

All About Biology by Robert Winston (Dorling Kindersley)

Amazing Science: Plants by Sally Hewitt (Wayland)

Cycles in Nature: Plant Life by Theresa Greenaway (Wayland)

Moving Up with Science: Plants by Peter Riley (Franklin Watts)

The Big Countdown: 10,000 Poisonous Plants in the World by Paul Rockett (Franklin Watts)

WEBSITES

PowerKids Press has developed an online list of websites related to the subject of this book. This site is updated regularly. Please use this link to access the list:

www.powerkidslinks.com/tyss/plants

INDEX

*Your carrot, lettuce, and leek may grow shoots and roots, but they will not grow any new vegetables. If your garlic clove grows shoots and roots, try planting it and it may grow a whole new garlic bulb, which you can eat.